Rusty

The Forgotten
Fire Engine

By **Joe Fisher**
Illustrations By **Jaye Boswell**

Will, Lila, & Jack
Enjoy Rusty!
Jaye Boswell

Joe Fisher

We would like to thank family: Ellen Thompson, Barrie Dewane and the Chuck Thompson boys, friends: Rolly and Bev Boorman, Lynn Beaty, Susan Logar Brody, Cara Davis, and Christopher Fous, and colleagues: Eric Bareto, Veronica Yager, Steve Turner and Dwight Stagg for their encouragement, support and contributions to making Rusty come to life.

Rusty The Forgotten Fire Engine

Printed in the United States of America
by
Creative Printing Services Inc., 2017

ISBN 978-0-9905678-1-3

Angler Publishing
PO Box 129
Sanibel Island, Florida 33957
www.AnglerPublishing.com

First Edition
10 9 8 7 6 5 4 3 2

Joe Fisher dedicates this book to his daughter Jane for whom the story was created and who never tired of hearing that all the flowers came back to life.

For Jane

Jaye Boswell dedicates this book to all the brave firefighters who man the fire engines and risk their lives saving children and adults, animals, buildings and forests.

For Firefighters

Once, many years but not so long ago, the people who lived in Someport-by-the-Sea decided they needed a new fire engine.

It all started one day when someone just happened to say to no one in particular "I think our town needs a new fire engine."

"You know that's a very good idea," said a person who overheard.

"I think so too," added a third person standing nearby.

Soon buying a new fire engine seemed to be all the people in town talked about until eventually everyone thought it was the right thing to do.

At the next town meeting, the Mayor Himself rose to speak to all the townspeople. "I have an idea," he said. "As a matter of public safety, I think it is time for the city of Someport-by-the-Sea to buy a new fire engine."

"Brilliant,"
said the City Fathers.

"Wise Decision,"
said the City Mothers.

"That's why he's our mayor,"
said the City Council.

So the next day the Mayor Himself called the Fire Chief into his office. "Go buy a new fire engine," he told the Fire Chief in a very mayorly way. And the Fire Chief did just that.

The Chief looked and he shopped and he shopped and he looked until at last he found just what all the firemen wanted – a brand new, bright red fire engine.

When the Chief took the fire engine back to the firehouse all the firemen agreed it was the most beautiful shade of red they had ever seen and that they would look very heroic riding to a fire on it.

They all agreed too that the fire engine had everything they would ever need to put out fires.

To help speed them to a fire, the fire engine had:

A bell that went

Ding, Dong
    Dingity-dong

(As if to say)
Hold on. I won't be long

Horns that went

Beep, Beep
    Beepity-beep

Here I come. Get off the street

Lights that went
Blink, Blink
    Blinkity-blink

I'll be there as quick as a wink

A siren that went
Woo-ah, Woo-ah
    Whoop, Whoop,
       Woo-ay

I'm on my way. I'll save the day.

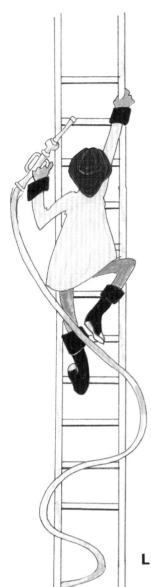

At the fire the firemen unload all the equipment and start to fight the fire.

Ladders go

Up Up
Uppity-up

(As if to say)
Come down with me.
No need to jump.

Axes go

Chop Chop
Chopity-
chop

Cut out the flames.
Make them stop.

Hoses go

Squirt Squirt
Squirty-
squirt

The fire's out. I've done my work.

And, of course, like all good fire engines it had a fire dog who went:

Bark, Bark
      Barkity-bark

Look at me. My Name is Sparks!

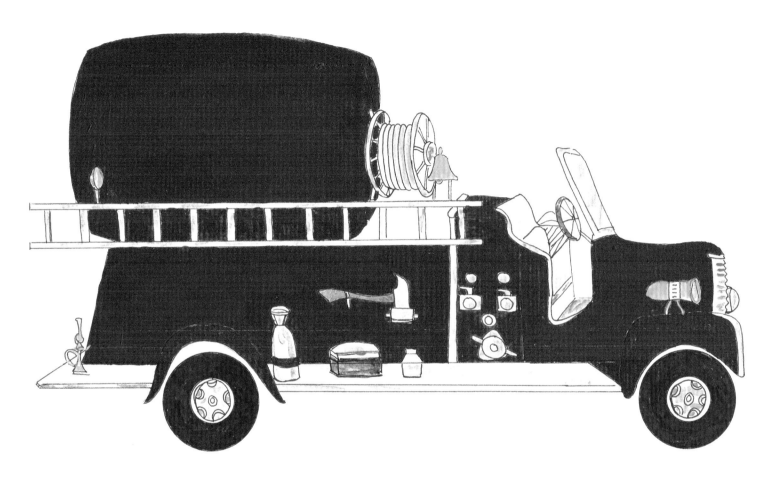

But by far the most wonderful thing about the new fire engine was the big round, bright red water tank it carried on its back right between the ladders. The tank was always filled to the very top with water so the fire engine was ready to fight a fire any time of the day or night.

Because the fire engine was painted bright red and because it was always ready to fight fires, the firemen just naturally started to call it Reddy for short. The name caught on and it wasn't long before all the boys and girls, townspeople and even the Mayor Himself were calling the fire engine Reddy.

When the fire engine zoomed through the streets of Someport-by-the-Sea on its way to a fire, with lights blinking, bell clanging, horn beeping, and siren wailing, all the people would say "There goes Reddy – ready again."

When the children in town saw Reddy
drive down the street, they would run
and dance alongside singing

Reddy, Reddy red and bright
Standing guard both day and night
In the dark and in the light
Reddy, Reddy has fires to fight

The boys and girls of Someport-by-the-Sea loved Reddy. Whenever there was a class trip they only wanted to go to the fire station. "May we go to the fire station today to see Reddy?" they asked their teachers.

At the fire house they climbed all over the fire engine, took turns sitting behind the wheel, beeping the horn, ringing the bell, blowing the siren and pretending they were flying along the streets of Someport-by-the-Sea on their way to fight a fire.

All the firemen were very proud of Reddy and they worked hard to keep him clean and shiny. Reddy's driver, Fireman Jim, was especially fond of the new fire engine and he worked night and day to make sure Reddy was always bright and clean and ready at a minute's notice to go fight a fire.

One afternoon a boy named Mike came to the fire station. "I want to be a fireman when I grow up," he announced to Jim.

"Well you have to be very brave and you will have to work very hard," Jim replied.

"I **AM** very brave," said Mike, "and I'm a **VERY** hard worker." "In that case," Jim said, "why don't you help me keep Reddy clean and shiny?"

Mike liked the idea. Every day after school he hurried to the fire station where he helped Fireman Jim wash and polish Reddy.

Mike was at the fire station so often that the other firemen started to call him Deputy Fire Chief Mike. They even gave him a fireman's hat and coat to wear.

Jim would look at his little friend and say with a smile, "He's the hardest working fireman in town."

Every year on the 4th of July the town of Someport-by-the-Sea had a big parade. In the early morning before the ball games, the swimming and the picnics and especially before the fireworks all the townspeople came to town to get the very best seats to see the parade.

Some sat on blankets, some sat on chairs and some even climbed trees to get the best view. They lined Main St. for as far as the eye could see and a little bit farther than that even.

Then they waited and they waited and they waited even longer still. Finally, when it seemed that the children could not stand to wait another minute longer they heard a noise in the distance.

The sound grew louder and louder
until down the street came the parade.

First came the soldiers carrying the
flags.
Then came the marching bands and
baton twirlers.
Followed by the boy scouts and girl
scouts and floats of every kind
and color.
There were boys and girls on bikes,
men on stilts and juggling
clowns,
Horses, carts and vehicles of all
descriptions,
Police cars, ambulances, street
sweepers and every truck the
city owned.

And, of course, that year Reddy lead the
parade. Jim drove Reddy, Mike sat next
to him, and the Mayor Himself rode on
top where everyone could see him.

But the next year when it was time for the big parade the new snow plow the town just bought was at the front of the line and the Mayor Himself was seated on top. Reddy was behind the soldiers, the bands, the scouts and the floats but ahead of the police cars, ambulances and all the trucks the city owned.

The year after that the town bought a new dump truck and that year it led the parade. Then the next year the new road grader came first and the year after that the new ambulance was in the lead.

Every year Reddy moved farther and farther back in the parade until he was at the very end of the line. Nobody called Reddy's name any more. No boys and girls ran along beside.

As the years went by Reddy began to look old and tired. The bell barely rang (Clank), the siren (Whoaaa) and the horn (beep - beep) were hard to hear, the lights weren't bright and the water tank faded to a dull, pale red and was covered with rust spots.

Fireman Jim polished and polished but no matter how hard he worked he could not seem to make Reddy shine like it did when it was new.

As the years went by too the boys and girls in Someport-by-the-Sea lost interest in Reddy. Fewer and fewer came to see the fire engine and Jim. At last even Mike the Deputy Fire Chief grew too old to be interested in fire engines any more. One day he just stopped coming to see Reddy and to help Jim polish the big red water tank.

After awhile the people in the town began to talk. "Maybe we should get a new fire engine," they said.

"Reddy doesn't look so ready anymore," commented several.

"He's just too old," everyone agreed.

Even the Mayor Himself thought it would be a good idea to buy a new fire engine to replace Reddy.

"But you can't do that to Reddy, Mayor," protested Fireman Jim. The Mayor Himself just laughed a mean little laugh.

"Look at that fire engine," he said to Jim.

"Reddy? Don't you mean Rusty? Ha, Ha, Ha," he snickered.

Several people over heard the Mayor's comment and they thought he was very clever and they laughed too. They told all their friends the Mayor's joke. The new name caught on and from then on Reddy was known as Rusty.

Now moms and dads laughed when they saw Rusty go by. "Ha Ha, there goes that broken down old fire engine," everyone hooted. "Rusty's not ready anymore," they jeered.

Boys and girls still ran along beside the fire engine but they didn't dance and laugh as they once had. Now they sang as they ran

Rusty, Rusty, old and slow
The fire's out before you show
Rusty, Rusty time to go

Jim and Rusty were heartbroken.

It was always hot during the summer in Someport-by-the-Sea, but that summer it was especially hot. It was a real heat wave.

Day after day the sun beamed down from the sky scorching everyone and everything in town.

Even in the early morning, it was too hot to go outside. Boys and girls did not want to leave the house to play baseball or ride bikes or go to the lake to swim even. Dogs and cats just laid in the shade and panted.

The townspeople had never seen anything like it before.
"Phew! It sure is hot," they said.
"Why, I've never seen anything like this before," they all exclaimed.

To make matters worse, it didn't rain at all that summer. It was a real drought. Day after day there wasn't a single cloud in the sky -- nothing to block the sunshine, no shade and no rain to cool the air.

The townspeople of Someport-by-the-Sea had never seen anything like this before either. "Why I've never seen it this dry before," they all said.

"I sure do wish it would rain," said one woman.

"We need a real gully washer," said a man.

After a while the grass and the lawns all across town turned brown, the leaves on the trees curled up and turned yellow and the flowers in the flower pots and the gardens by every house in Someport-by-the-Sea wilted and died.

On the 4th of July that year, Rusty and Jim, alone and forgotten, were at the back of the parade as usual. No one seemed to notice as they drove down the street. Some people even got up to leave when they saw the little red fire engine because they knew the parade was almost over.

Jim and Reddy were **very** sad and **very** lonely. Jim hung his head and gave a big sad sigh as he drove along. Rusty seemed to sag, as if all the air had gone out of his tires. The farther they drove the lower Jim hung his head, the louder he sighed, the more Rusty sagged and the slower they went.

As they neared the finish of the parade where only a few people still stayed to watch, Rusty and Jim passed a man standing beside the road holding hands with two children. When he saw Rusty he almost didn't recognize the forlorn fire engine. Then suddenly the man broke into a big wide grin.

He quickly lifted the children to his shoulders so they could see the fire engine passing by.

"Kids," he said. "See that little red fire engine? That's the best fire engine there ever was."

"**It is Daddy?**" asked the children.

"Yes it is. When I was a boy about your ages I took care of that fire engine. I kept it clean and shiny."

"**You did Daddy?**" the children asked.

"Yes I really did," the man named Mike said.

Fireman Jim heard someone talking and shyly glanced over at the crowd. He saw two children sitting on their father's shoulders way above the crowd.

Then he stopped and took a longer look and he started to smile. Jim waved to get the man's attention. He waved and waved so hard it seemed as if he would fly away.

"Deputy Fire Chief Mike," Jim yelled.

Mike and the children waved back. "Why hello Jim," Mike yelled.

Rusty was so happy to see Deputy Fire Chief Mike he rose up on his wheels. His grill turned up in a smile. And he puffed out his water tank.

People in the crowd began to notice.

"Will you look at Rusty," one man exclaimed.

"Why he looks like he did when he was new," said a woman.

"Hi, Rusty," shouted a boy.

"Yoo-hoo, Rusty," waved a girl.

The more the crowd noticed the more Rusty swelled until he was ready to burst with pride.

Then all at once it happened. One of Rusty's rust spots popped. Water squirted out, shooting high into the air. Another popped. Then another and another until Rusty looked like a big red watering can.

All the children, moms, dads, dogs, policemen, the marching band and even the Mayor Himself were hit by the spray. It was cool and wet and wonderful.

Everyone smiled and laughed and followed Rusty down the street, dancing in the rusty rain.

The water ran down the streets, into the gutters, over the curbs and out onto the brown, dry lawns.

Steam rose from the sizzling streets. Boys and girls splashed in the cool puddles. The grass gulped up the wetness and all the lawns turned green again. And all the flowers came back to life.

Rusty and Jim had saved the summer.

The next year the town did buy a brand new fire engine after all. It was big, bright red and had all the latest tools to fight fires. The firemen looked very heroic riding on it while rushing to a fire.

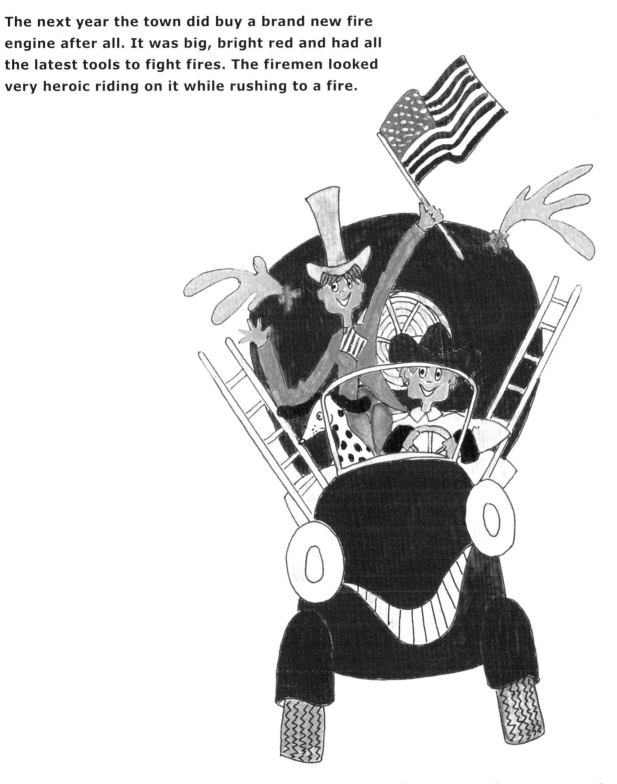

But that year and every year after that, on the 4th of July, Rusty, the water sprinkler truck, led the big parade. Mike drove and the Mayor Himself rode on top.

Joe Fisher is a twenty-three year resident of Sanibel Island. He received advanced degrees from Tufts and Harvard Universities in Sociology and Public Health respectively. Joe shares with Jaye a love of children and the environment. He coached Sanibel Little League and spent a decade as a volunteer docent in the J. N. "Ding" Darling Wildlife Refuge.

Joe's writing career is wide ranging and eclectic. He has written more than twenty scientific papers and invited chapters as well as four books including two for the trade about serial murder and near death experiences.

As the father of two children Joe is passionate about the importance of loved ones reading to young children on a frequent basis. *Rusty the Forgotten Fire Engine* is his first children's book and is the written version of a story he created and told his children when they were young.

Jaye Boswell, a thirty-five year Sanibel Island resident, graduated from the University of Miami with a BA in Art Education. For twenty-two years she taught in the Lee County (Florida) School System where she was named Visual Arts Teacher of the Year in 2004.

During the 1989-1990 school year Jaye combined art with environmental education by having her students draw ducks in a wildlife setting. From this class project the Federal Junior Duck Stamp emerged. Judged annually at the J. N. "Ding" Darling Wildlife Refuge, the annual program has forty thousand entries a year from across the United States and U.S. Territories.

Although retired from teaching Jaye remains active as an artist creating work that reflects her love of art, the environment and children.